The
Christmas Star's
Big Shine

Text copyright © Alexa Tewkesbury 2005
Illustrations copyright © CWR 2005
Published 2005 by CWR, Waverley Abbey House, Waverley Lane, Farnham, Surrey, GU9 8EP, England.
The right of Alexa Tewkesbury to be identified as the author of this work has been asserted by her in accordance with the Copyright, Designs and Patents Act 1988.

Concept development, editing, design and production by CWR.
Illustrated by Steve Boulter.
Printed in China by 1010 Printing International Ltd.
ISBN 1-85345-355-2

National Distributors

UK: (and countries not listed below)
CWR, Waverley Abbey House, Waverley Lane, Farnham, Surrey GU9 8EP. Tel: (01252) 784700 Outside UK +44 1252 784700

AUSTRALIA: CMC Australasia, PO Box 519, Belmont, Victoria 3216. Tel: (03) 5241 3288

CANADA: Cook Communications Ministries, PO Box 98, 55 Woodslee Avenue, Paris, Ontario. Tel: 1800 263 2664

GHANA: Challenge Enterprises of Ghana, PO Box 5723, Accra. Tel: (021) 222437/223249 Fax: (021) 226227

HONG KONG: Cross Communications Ltd, 1/F, 562A Nathan Road, Kowloon. Tel: 2780 1188 Fax: 2770 6229

INDIA: Crystal Communications, 10-3-18/4/1, East Marredpalli, Secunderabad – 500026, Andhra Pradesh. Tel/Fax: (040) 27737145

KENYA: Keswick Books and Gifts Ltd, PO Box 10242, Nairobi. Tel: (02) 331692/226047 Fax: (02) 728557

MALAYSIA: Salvation Book Centre (M) Sdn Bhd, 23 Jalan SS 2/64, 47300 Petaling Jaya, Selangor. Tel: (03) 78766411/78766797 Fax: (03) 78757066/78756360

NEW ZEALAND: CMC Australasia, PO Box 36015, Lower Hutt. Tel: 0800 449 408 Fax: 0800 449 049

NIGERIA: FBFM, Helen Baugh House, 96 St Finbarr's College Road, Akoka, Lagos. Tel: (01) 7747429/4700218/825775/827264

PHILIPPINES: OMF Literature Inc, 776 Boni Avenue, Mandaluyong City. Tel: (02) 531 2183 Fax: (02) 531 1960

SINGAPORE: Armour Publishing Pte Ltd, Block 203A Henderson Road, 11–06 Henderson Industrial Park, Singapore 159546. Tel: 6 276 9976 Fax: 6 276 7564

SOUTH AFRICA: Struik Christian Books, 80 MacKenzie Street, PO Box 1144, Cape Town 8000. Tel: (021) 462 4360 Fax: (021) 461 3612

SRI LANKA: Christombu Books, 27 Hospital Street, Colombo 1. Tel: (01) 433142/328909

TANZANIA: CLC Christian Book Centre, PO Box 1384, Mkwepu Street, Dar es Salaam. Tel/Fax: (022) 2119439

USA: Cook Communications Ministries, PO Box 98, 55 Woodslee Avenue, Paris, Ontario, Canada. Tel: 1800 263 2664

ZIMBABWE: Word of Life Books, Shop 4, Memorial Building, 35 S Machel Avenue, Harare. Tel: (04) 781305 Fax: (04) 774739

For email addresses, visit the CWR website: www.cwr.org.uk

CWR is a registered charity – number 294387

The Christmas Star's Big Shine

by Alexa Tewkesbury

Illustrations by Steve Boulter

The night was still. Little Star flickered sleepily in the velvet sky.

Suddenly –

'Wake up!'

He opened his eyes with a start. An angel was nudging him with a shimmer-white wing.
'Come on, rise and shine,' the angel chivvied. 'You've got an important job to do.'
'Have I?' whispered Little Star.
'A very special baby boy is about to be born in Bethlehem,' announced the angel.
'He's the Son of God, and He'll bring happiness to people all over the world.'
'Really?' murmured Little Star.
'Really,' said the angel. 'His name will be Jesus, and God wants *you* to let everyone know He's here.'
'Me?' gasped Little Star.
'Yes, you,' said the angel. 'You'd better get a move on.'

Little Star looked worried.
'But where do I go?' he asked.
'Bethlehem,' the angel replied as he flew off into the night. 'He'll be born in a stable there.'
'And how do I tell people?' called Little Star.

'Simple,' the angel called back. 'You just shine.'

Little Star thought for a moment.
'If God wants me to shine, I'll be the shiniest star in the whole universe,' he twinkled. 'Shining's what I do.'
Then he took a deep breath and –

'WHEEEEE!'

He shot off through the velvet sky, whizzing over fields and forests, across rivers and streams.
'Little Star coming through. Got an important job to do!'

Little Star zipped over swirling seas and flat, dusty plains. He was just zooming across a hot, steamy jungle when a cheeky voice said,

'You're in a hurry.'

Little Star called down,

'Can't stop. Got to fly. On a mission to light up the sky!'

'What for?' asked the voice.

'To tell everyone about God's new baby,' replied Little Star proudly. 'Are we in Bethlehem?'

'Not really,' said the voice. 'This is Africa. But I'll help you find the way.'

Little Star peered through the tangle of trees and creepers
straight into the eyes of –

A MONKEY.
'I won't be any trouble,' Monkey said. He scrambled to the top
of a very tall tree, grasped Little Star's gleaming tail and –

WHEEESH!
They scooted off through the velvet sky.
They flashed across a huge ocean and skimmed over a rich, leafy rainforest.

'Looks like fun,' rumbled a voice.

Little Star called down,

'Can't stop. Got to fly. On a mission to light up the sky!'

'Can I help?' purred the voice.

Monkey chirped, 'Is this Bethlehem?'

'Oh no,' replied the voice. 'This is India. Will that do?'

'Not tonight,' said Little Star. 'I've got to tell everyone about God's new baby.'.

'Mind if I join you?' asked the voice.

Little Star and monkey peeped through the juicy green leaves and found themselves face to face with –

A TIGER.
'I'll be quiet as a mouse,' he promised.
So Tiger took hold of Monkey, Monkey grasped Little Star's tail
and –

SWISSSH!!
They dashed away through the velvet sky.
They soared over mighty mountains, then scurried across
shadowy forests of thick bamboo.

'Got room for one more?' asked a hopeful voice.
Little Star called down,
'Can't stop. Got to fly. On a mission to light up the sky!'
'Is it dangerous?' enquired the voice.
'Not dangerous,' said Little Star, 'but very important. Is this Bethlehem?'
'Good gracious, no,' answered the voice, 'this is China. Bethlehem's that way. Shall I show you?'
Little Star, Monkey and Tiger all squinted down and there, peeking back up at them was –

A PANDA.

'Yes, please,' cried Little Star. 'I've got to tell everyone about God's new baby.'

So Panda took hold of Tiger, Tiger held onto Monkey, Monkey grasped Little Star's tail and –

PHIZZZZ!!
They rushed off through the velvet sky.
Faster and faster they flew. Then suddenly –

'Look out!'
An angel shot out of the sky in front of them.
'We're going to crash!' squealed Monkey.
Little Star shuddered and juddered and screeched and –

Stopped. Just in time.

'Terribly sorry,' said the angel, 'but I've got to spread some amazing news so I can't hang about.'

Little Star's eyes opened wide.

'Has Jesus been born?' he asked.

The angel looked puzzled. 'Only just. How did you know?'

'*I've* got to spread the news too,' Little Star grinned.

The angel pointed down to a small, scruffy stable.

'Jesus is asleep in there with His mother, Mary, and Joseph, her husband,' he smiled. 'One day He'll rescue people from all the bad things in their lives and bring them close to God.'

Little Star beamed. 'So this must be where I'm supposed to shine.'

'Definitely,' said the angel. 'Anyway, must dash. I've got to give some shepherds the good news.' Then winking at Little Star, the angel added 'Enjoy your Big Shine', and flew away.

'My Big Shine,' thought Little Star. Then –

'Oh no!' he cried. 'Supposing I'm too small. God wants me to shine brightly enough to let everyone know about His wonderful new baby. But what if I can't? What if nobody notices?'

'Of course everyone will notice,' replied Monkey. '*We* all noticed you, didn't we?'

So Little Star closed his eyes, puffed out his chest and began to shine as he'd never shone before.
At first he only glimmered.

But then the glimmer grew into a glow …

and the glow began to beam …

and soon the beam became a gleam …

and all of a sudden Little Star burst into the most dazzling shine of his life!

'Am I doing it?' he shouted.

'Yes!' shrieked the animals. 'Look!'

Far, far away, three wise-looking men were pointing at Little Star. Then they each picked up a present for the baby Jesus and set off to find Him, following Little Star's glaring trail.

'They all want to see Jesus,' cried Monkey, 'and they'll find Him because of you, Little Star.'
Some shepherds were gazing at Little Star too. His radiant light guided them right to the stable door.

Little Star glittered with glee, and the velvet sky blazed in the brilliant light of the biggest shine the world would ever see.